Top Cat

Lois Ehlert

SCRITCH
SCRATCH

Harcourt Brace & Company
San Diego   New York   London
Printed in Hong Kong

O-KA-LEE
O-KA-LEE

I'm top cat.
Pet me, I'll purr.

I guard this place
in my coat of fur.

PURR
URR
PURR
URR

Boring job! Never see a
Nothing much happens
in this dull house.

mouse.

CREEEK
SLAM
THUMP
SCRATCH
SCRATCH

Who let you in?
One cat's
enough.

ME-OW
SCRATCH
SCRATCH
SCRATCH
ME-OW

SNIFF
SNIFF

I don't want to share my stuff.

SWISH
SWISH

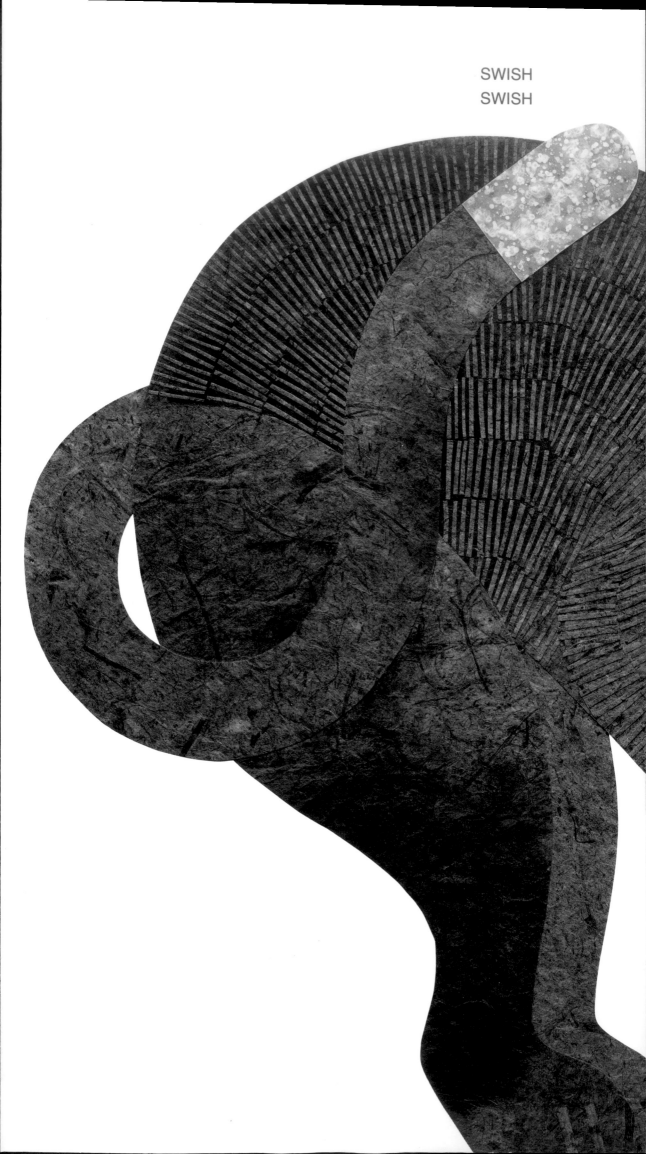

SWISH
SWISH

Go away, cat!

GRRRR
HISS
HISS

You've
invaded
my space.

SWISH
SWISH

CHEEP
CHEEP
CHEEP

GRRRR
HISS
HISS

And I don't like your cute little face.

SWISH
SWISH

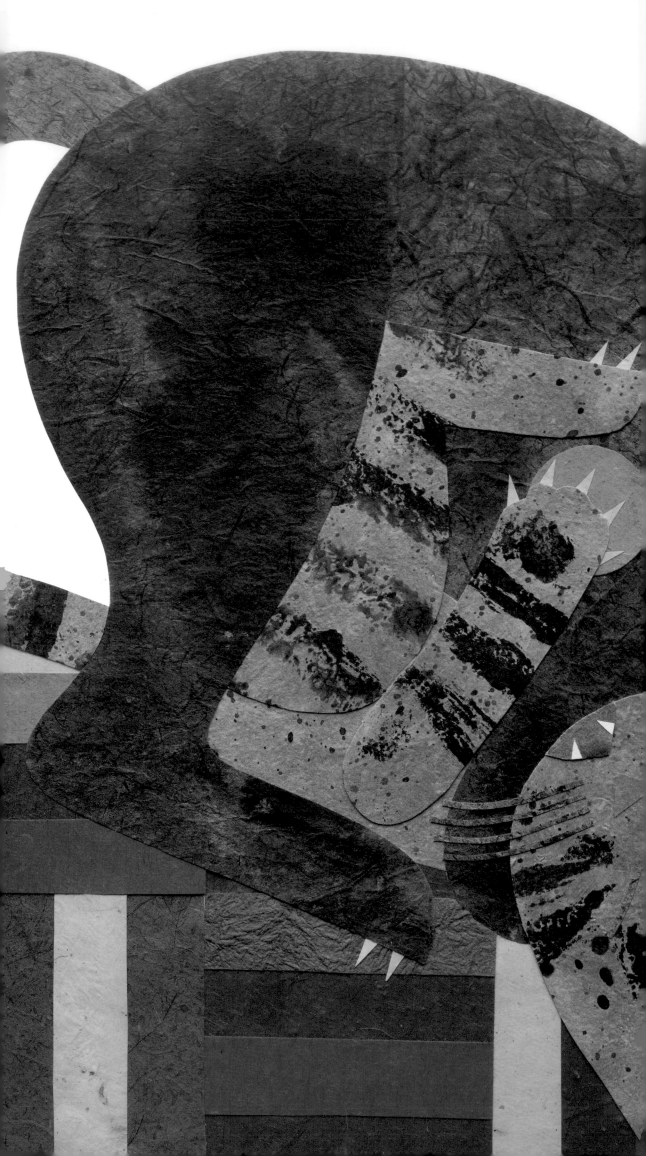

I'll fight you and bite you behind the ear. Get the message? I'm boss around here.

Well, you're here
to stay.
I can see that.

SCRATCH
SCRATCH

Guess I'm
stuck with you,
striped cat.

SWISH

JINGLE
JINGLE

THUNK

But
there's
more to do
than eat
and sleep.

JINGLE
JINGLE

WHIZ

Keep your green eyes open. Watch me leap!

Bounce on
the couch.
Leave
lots of
hair.

Eat leaves till
the plants are bare.

CHOMP

CHOMP

Drink from the sink when

DRIP

company's there.

Dance on
the table
with the
silverware.

JINGLE
JINGLE

CLINK
CLANK

Door's
left open?
Go get
some
fresh air.

JINGLE
JINGLE

WHOOSH

Test your claws.
Give birds a good scare.

JINGLE
JINGLE

Time to eat! You'd better decide.

Will you come in or stay outside?

WHAT
CHEER
WIT
WIT
WIT

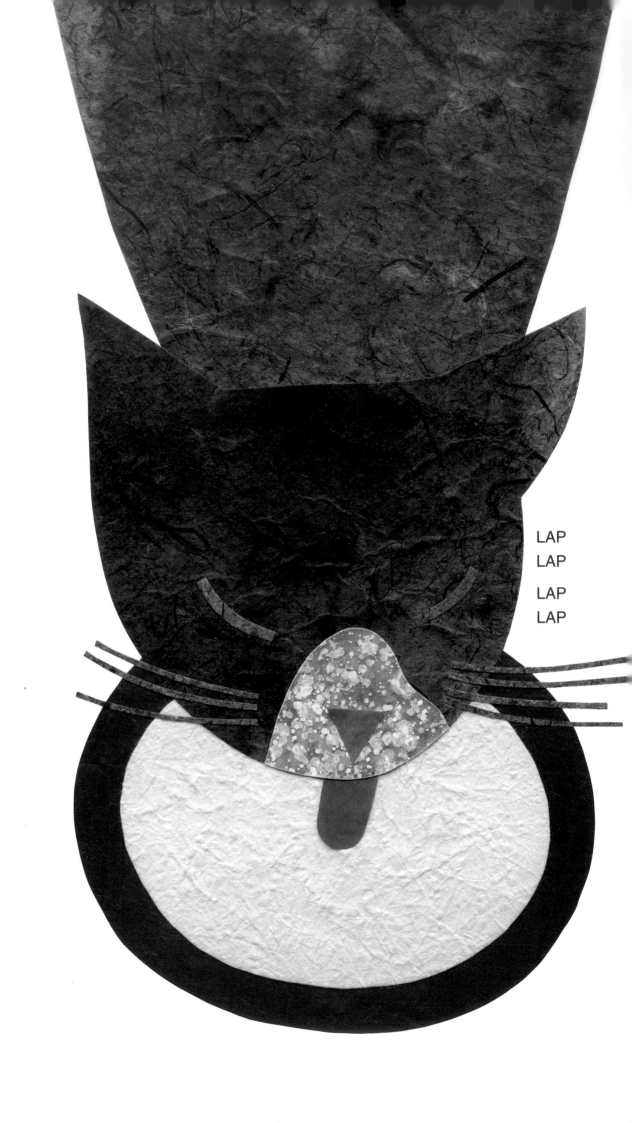

LAP
LAP

LAP
LAP

Welcome back!
Let's drink milk
in our furs.
No hisses,
no scratches,
no bites.

Just
purrs.

LIP
LIP

LIP
LIP

For Shirley and Don

Library of Congress Cataloging-in-Publication Data
Ehlert, Lois.
Top cat/Lois Ehlert [author and illustrator].
p. cm.
Summary: The top cat in a household is reluctant to
accept the arrival of a new kitten but decides to share
various survival secrets with it.
ISBN 0-15-201739-9
1. Cats—Juvenile fiction. [1. Cats—Fiction.